CHARLIE THE PUPPY

Abigail Pizer

MACMILLAN CHILDREN'S BOOKS

Thank you,
Bishop and Baptist

First published 1988 by
MACMILLAN CHILDREN'S BOOKS
A division of Macmillan Publishers Limited
London and Basingstoke
Associated companies throughout the world

British Library Cataloguing in Publication Data
Pizer, Abigail
 Charlie the puppy. — (Nettlepatch Farm series).
 I. Title   II. Series
 823'.914[J]   PZ7

 ISBN 0-333-44737-9

Printed in Hong Kong

It is spring-time on Nettlepatch Farm.
On the farm live Mr Potter, Mrs Potter and
their little daughter Amy.

Everyone on the farm is busy.
The ducks are busy looking after their new ducklings.
The pigs are busy with their piglets.

The goats are busy with their kids.
And the sheep are busy with their lambs.

Amy is back at school and Mr and Mrs Potter are both busy on the farm.
Everyone has lots to do except Charlie – Amy's new puppy.
He sits all alone in the kitchen wondering why no one will take any notice of him.

Even Billingsgate the cat ignores him.
So Charlie decides to go outside, hoping to
find someone to play with.

The ducks are the first animals Charlie sees.
When the ducks see Charlie they all start to quack!
Charlie wags his tail and barks.

The ducks quack louder and louder.
They don't like Charlie being so close.
The mother ducks guide their ducklings to the middle of the
pond.

Charlie doesn't understand why the ducks swam away.
He only wants to be friends.

Charlie makes his way to the pigsty.
He is sure the piglets will play with him.

But the piglets are busy feeding. They don't even notice
Charlie.

The mother pig sees Charlie and warns him off with a loud grunt.
Charlie slinks away – he knows he is not wanted here either.

In the orchard he sees the two baby goats. They are playing together and they want Charlie to join in.

Their mother doesn't, and she chases him away.

Charlie is very sad – but he brightens up when he sees a whole field full of sheep and lambs.
Surely *they* will want to play with him?

No, the sheep definitely do not want to play with Charlie.
They are frightened of him and run to the farthest corners of the field.

Poor Charlie is so fed up.
Why will no one play with him?
He does not even notice the two angry geese
as he passes right through their family of
little goslings.

The goose and gander chase Charlie into the milk shed, flapping their wings and hissing and honking as loud as they can.

Charlie rushes into the dark barn and crashes into a milk churn which tumbles on its side spilling milk all over the floor.

The geese hurry back to their goslings.
Charlie stays in the barn, trembling.
He knows he has been naughty.

It is not long before Mrs Potter comes into the barn to fetch some milk.
There is Charlie, covered in milk and mud and looking very sorry for himself.

Mrs Potter takes him into the kitchen and gives him a good
warm soapy bath in an old tin basin.

Then she wraps Charlie in a towel and sets him down in front of the stove to dry.

After a while Amy comes home from school
and makes a big fuss of him.
Charlie is happy now and wags his tail
madly.
He is so pleased to see Amy again.

Nettlepatch Farm